I Wish I Had Freckles Like Abby
Quisiera tener pecas como Abby

Written by / Escrito por Kathryn Heling and Deborah Hembrook
Illustrated by / Ilustrado por Bonnie Adamson
Translated by / Traducido por Eida de la Vega

To all my little kindergarten friends with freckles, especially Abby!
— Love from Mrs. Hembrook
XO

To children everywhere and to feeling special just the way you are!
— KEH

To Jenny and Steffie, always, freckles or not!
— BCA

Text Copyright ©2007 by Kathryn Heling and Deborah Hembrook
Illustration Copyright ©2007 by Bonnie Adamson
Translation Copyright ©2007 by Raven Tree Press

Heling, Kathryn and Hembrook, Deborah.

I wish I had freckles like Abby/written by Kathryn Heling and Deborah Hembrook; illustrated by Bonnie Adamson; translated by Eida de la Vega = Quisiera tener pecas como Abby/escrito por Kathryn Heling and Deborah Hembrook; ilustrado por Bonnie Adamson; traducción al español de Eida de la Vega.–1st ed.–McHenry, IL: Raven Tree Press, 2007.

p.; cm.

Text in English and Spanish.

Summary: Rosa goes to elaborate and comical lengths to get freckles like Abby. She realizes she might have something that is just as desirable as the longed-for freckles. Rosa gains appreciation of her own uniqueness.

ISBN-10–0-9724973-8-2 hardcover   ISBN 10–0-9770906-6-3 paperback
ISBN-13–978-0-9724973-8-1   ISBN 13–978-0-9770906-6-2

1. Freckles–Juvenile fiction. 2. Friendship–Juvenile fiction.
3. Self-Esteem–Juvenile fiction. 4. Bilingual books–English and Spanish. 5. [Spanish language materials–books.] I. Illust. Adamson, Bonnie. II. Title. III. Quisiera tener pecas como Abby.

LCCN–2003093676
CIP

Printed in China
10 9 8 7 6 5 4 3 2 1
first edition

I Wish I Had Freckles Like Abby
Quisiera tener pecas como Abby

Written by / Escrito por Kathryn Heling and Deborah Hembrook
Illustrated by / Ilustrado por Bonnie Adamson
Translated by / Traducido por Eida de la Vega

Raven Tree Press
A DIVISION OF DELTA SYSTEMS CO., INC.

I wish I had freckles like Abby.
Her freckles make her look beautiful.

Quisiera tener pecas como Abby.
¡Se ve muy bonita con ellas!

4

Abby and I like to draw.
I put freckles on the picture of me.
I love freckles!

A Abby y a mí nos gusta dibujar.
Yo me hice un retrato y le puse pecas.
¡Me encantan las pecas!

I used my sister's make-up to dot freckles on my face.
Everything was a mess.

Con el maquillaje de mi hermana, me dibujé pecas en toda la cara.
Fue un desastre.

8

I cleaned all day.
I'll never do that again!

Me pasé todo el día limpiándolo.
¡No lo volveré a hacer!

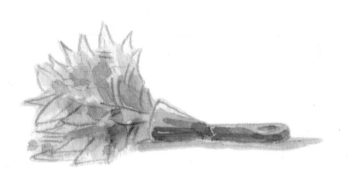

11

Paint splashed me on the playground.
I had a million tiny freckles.

La pintura salpicó cuando jugábamos.
Parecía que tenía un millón de pecas diminutas.

13

14

My teacher made me wash them off.

La maestra me obligó a limpiarme la cara.

Last week, I made chocolate pudding freckles.
They were delicious.

La semana pasada, me dibujé pecas con natilla de de chocolate.
Estaban deliciosas.

Then the neighbor's dog licked them.
I'll never do that again!

Entonces, el perro del vecino vino a lamerlas.
¡No lo volveré a hacer!

Once, I landed in a puddle.
I had mud freckles everywhere.

Un día, aterricé en un charco.
Tenía pecas de barro por todas partes.

Mom didn't think it was funny.

A mamá no le pareció gracioso.

When I got chickenpox, I really did have freckles!

Cuando tuve varicela, ¡me salieron pecas de verdad!

They were red and itchy.
I never want freckles like that again!

Eran rojas y me escocían.
¡No quiero tener unas pecas como ésas!

I still wish I had freckles like Abby!
But Abby wishes she had glasses like me!

Todavía quiero tener pecas como Abby.
¡Sin embargo, Abby quiere tener lentes como yo!

29

Imagine that!

¡Imagínate!

31

Vocabulary
English

freckles
beautiful
teacher
sister
chocolate
dog
mud
red
Mom
imagine

Vocabulario
Español

las pecas
bonita
la maestra
la hermana
el chocolate
el perro
el barro
rojas
la mamá
imagínate (imaginar)

32

32